ANACONDAS

THE SNAKE DISCOVERY LIBRARY

Sherie Bargar Linda Johnson

Photographer/Consultant: George Van Horn

Watermill Press
Mahwah, New Jersey

Library of Congress Cataloging in Publication Data

Bargar, Sherie, 1944-
  Anacondas.

  (The Snake discovery library)
  Includes index.
  Summary: An introduction to the physical
characteristics, habits, natural environment and
relationship to human beings of the various species
of anacondas.
  1. Anaconda—Juvenile literature. [1. Anaconda.
2. Snakes] I. Johnson, Linda, 1947-   . II. Van Horn,
George, ill.   III. Title.   IV. Series: Bargar, Sherie,
1944-   . Snake discovery library.
  QL666.063B36   1987   597.95   87-12672
  ISBN 0-86592-249-7

Title Photo:
Yellow Anaconda
Eunectes notaeus

TABLE OF CONTENTS

ANACONDAS

Giant **nonvenomous** anacondas, members of *Boidae* family, are among the world's largest snakes. These aquatic creatures have heavier bodies than other boas. Anacondas are as thick as a telephone pole and often over 20 feet long. Reports of 60 foot anacondas have never been proven. Spending nearly all of their lives in the water has earned them the common name of water boas. The name anaconda is believed to come from the South American Indians. The anaconda is a source of many myths which exaggerate its size and attacks on humans. Reports of these giant constrictors actually killing and eating humans are very few indeed.

Yellow Anaconda
Eunectes notaeus

WHERE THEY LIVE

Permanent bodies of water that are deep enough for the anaconda to **submerge** its entire monstrous body are the **habitat** of the giant snakes. The water is often murky and dark because the anaconda avoids swiftly moving, clear waters. Vegetation and a food supply are essential to their aquatic habitat. The swamps of South America are the most common homes of the giant creatures. While the anaconda lives almost entirely in the water, it is very capable of moving on land for short periods of time. Sometimes it may be spotted sunning itself on a fallen tree which stretches out over the water.

Yellow Anaconda
Eunectes notaeus

HOW THEY LOOK

The thick, heavy bodied Green Anacondas are olive with black spots. The Yellow Anaconda, however, is a smaller yellow snake with a complex pattern. The scales of all anacondas are smooth. A large anaconda may weigh over 200 pounds. A unique characteristic of the anaconda is the position of its eyes and nostrils. They are located on the head in much the same way as the crocodile's and alligator's eyes and nostrils. They allow the snake to **submerge** its head and body and leave only its eyes and nostrils out of the water. This unique physical trait helps the anaconda spot prey and still remain **camouflaged**.

Green Anaconda
Eunectes murinus

THEIR SENSES

Limited vision and the sense of smell are the strongest senses of the anaconda. The watertight eye covering allows the snake limited vision under water. The anaconda may sight movement in the water or on the bank of a river. To better determine what it has sighted it may utilize its sense of smell. The sense of feeling also helps the anaconda locate **prey**. The vibrations made by **intruders** both on land and water can be felt by the anaconda. The combination of sight, smell, and the sense of **vibrations** felt by the snake makes it an accurate and dangerous hunter.

Yellow Anaconda
Eunectes notaeus

Green Anaconda
Eunectes murinus

Notice how the eyes

and nose are alike.

American Alligator
Alligator mississippiensis

THE HEAD AND MOUTH

The large blunt-nosed head of the anaconda contains a mouth full of sharp, needle-like teeth which curve back toward the throat. The six rows of teeth are used to hold **prey** firmly during constriction. Powerful jaw muscles assist in swallowing **prey**. A windpipe extends from the throat to the front of the mouth to help the anaconda breathe as it swallows large **prey**. Swallowing really large **prey** may take several hours.

Yellow Anaconda
Eunectes notaeus

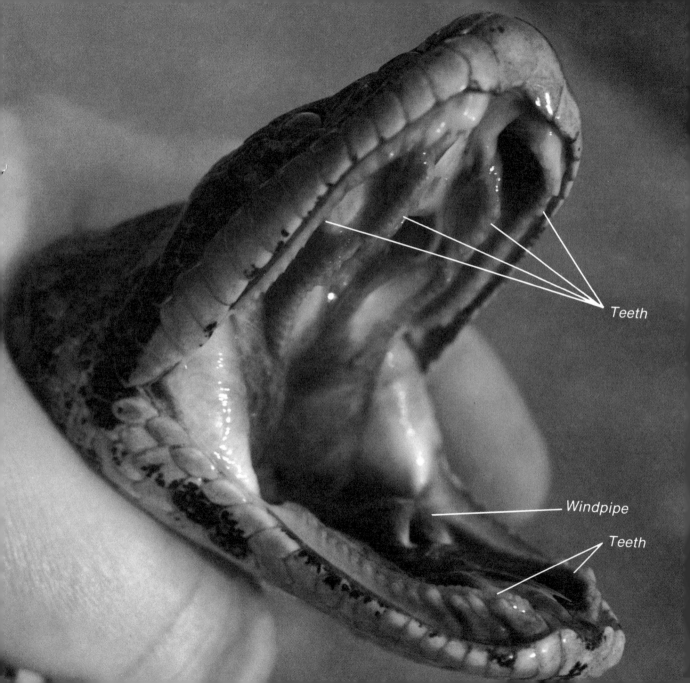

Teeth

Windpipe

Teeth

BABY ANACONDAS

Up to 50 young anacondas are born live in the summer or fall. Although the young vary in size, they are about 2 feet long at birth. The young snake will look like a miniature adult and will not change the color of its scales after birth. From birth, the young anacondas are excellent swimmers, are able to kill their own **prey** and defend themselves. A female anaconda may give birth twice a year.

Green Anaconda
Eunectes murinus

PREY

Prey at the water's edge may be ambushed by a hungry anaconda lying **submerged**. The same silent attack may befall a fish or duck in the water. The unsuspecting **prey** is seized by the curved teeth of the anaconda. As the **prey** struggles to free itself, it forces the snake's teeth deeper into its flesh. Once the grip is tightened, constriction begins. The snake wraps its body around the prey and tightens the grip each time the victim breathes out. Eventually the victim **suffocates**. The victim is swallowed whole and usually head first. A large anaconda may swallow sheep and small deer. Crocodiles have been known to eat anacondas.

Green Anaconda
Eunectes murinus

THEIR DEFENSE

Protective coloring **camouflages** the anaconda in murky water. Hiding is its greatest defense. It is too slow moving to run away from a potential enemy. The anaconda also tries to scare its enemy by imitating **venomous** snakes. It will hiss or fake a strike. It can also deliver a very painful bite that tears deeply into the flesh. An adult anaconda has few enemies because of its size.

Green Anaconda
Eunectes murinus

ANACONDAS AND PEOPLE

People are constantly expanding their civilized boundaries. The result is the loss of appropriate **habitats** for the giant snakes. The fashion industry still uses the leather skins of the giant snakes. Both of these behaviors make man the greatest enemy of the anaconda. Some people have purchased anacondas as pets. They are unaffectionate, but sometimes tame if purchased as a young snake. The anaconda has been known to live up to 20 years in the care of experts. Most only live a few short years in captivity.

GLOSSARY

camouflage (CAM ou flage) camouflaged, camouflages — The color of an animal's skin that matches the ground around it.

habitat (HAB i tat) habitats — A place where an animal lives.

intruder (in TRUD er) intruders — One who approaches another and is not welcome.

nonvenomous (non VEN om ous) — Does not cause sickness or death.

prey (PREY) — An animal hunted or killed by another animal for food.

submerge (sub MERGE) submerged — To cover with water.

suffocate (SUF fo cate) suffocates — To kill by not allowing an animal to breathe.

venomous (VEN om ous) — Causing sickness or death.

vibrate (VI brate) vibrations — To move back and forth.

INDEX